ECO RANGERS

RANGERS

WILDFIRE RESCUE

For the Noending family.

NEW FRONTIER PUBLISHING

American edition published in 2021
By New Frontier Publishing Europe Ltd
www.newfrontierpublishing.us

First published in the UK in 2020
by New Frontier Publishing Europe Ltd
Uncommon, 126 New King's Rd, Fulham, London SW6 4LZ
www.newfrontierpublishing.co.uk

ISBN: 978-1-913639-36-5

Illustrated by Aśka, www.askaillustration.com
Text copyright © 2020, 2021 Candice Lemon-Scott
Illustrations copyright © 2020, 2021 New Frontier Publishing
The moral right of the author has been asserted.

Distributed in the United States and Canada by Lerner Publishing Group Inc
241 First Avenue North, Minneapolis, MN 55401 USA
www.lernerbooks.com

Library of Congress Catalogue-in-Publication Data Available

Edited by Stephanie Stahl and Tasha Evans
Designed by Rachel Lawston

Printed in China

The paper and board used in this book
are made from wood from responsible sources.

FSC
www.fsc.org
MIX
From responsible
sources
FSC® C130668

1 3 5 7 9 10 8 6 4 2

ECO RANGERS
WILDFIRE RESCUE

CANDICE LEMON-SCOTT

Illustrated by Aśka

EBONY

Hi everyone, I'm Ebony! I'm twelve years old. I like spending time in nature, rescuing animals or riding my bike to go off on an adventure. I'm very independent, but sometimes I jump right in without thinking and that can get me into trouble! I love being an Eco Ranger because I get to solve mysteries!

JAY

I'm Jay, Ebony's best friend and next-door neighbor. I'm eleven years old. I like making jokes and have a bit of a sweet tooth... especially when it comes to cake! I also love nature and helping out at the wildlife hospital. Being an Eco Ranger is so much fun because I can look after animals and make sure they are safe.

Ebony and Jay trudged through the blackened scrub, the burned grass crunching under their feet. The two Eco Rangers, and best friends, were spending their Sunday in the bushland looking for any wildlife that might have been caught up in the recent wildfire. It had been hot and dry over the summer, with no rain, so a fire had easily started. The trees around them were black and it was eerily quiet without the usual bush sounds of birds, insects, and animals looking for food.

There was an orange haze in the air, and

it still smelled a little smoky. The scent of eucalyptus from the burned gum trees was strong. Ebony coughed. Jay covered his nose and stopped midway up a gravelly track. He wiped his sweaty forehead with the back of his oversized Eco Rangers T-shirt. Then he took off his glasses, removing the steam off them as well. It was harder work than they had expected, and it wasn't even the hottest part of the day yet.

"I need a rest," Jay said, spying a large log nearby.

"Good idea!" Ebony agreed.

The vets at the conservation center hospital, Doctor Battacharjee, who everyone called Doctor Bat for short, and Doctor Tan, were very busy caring for the wildlife that had been brought in after the fire. Some animals had burn injuries or had breathed in too much smoke. Others had lost their home or couldn't find any food. There could still be some more hurt or sick wildlife around though, so the Eco Rangers had been called in to search for any other animals that needed to be rescued, now that the area was safe. They had been given a carrier, a blanket, a sheet, gloves, and water bottles, in case they found any wildlife. Ebony put her backpack down while Jay placed his bag and the carrier on the ground beside him. So far, they hadn't found any animals that needed their help.

The Eco Rangers sat on the log. It wasn't very comfortable. They had to squeeze on either side of a stick jutting up from the log, and there were pieces of loose bark around them, but it was good to sit down and rest for a minute. One side, where their feet hung down, was still green and mossy while the other side was charred and black from the fire. Ebony tightened her dark, unruly hair that was held back in a ponytail with a bright green hairband. The hair under her cap was already wet with sweat.

"Time for a snack," Jay said, always thinking of his stomach.

"I'll get the water out, too. We don't want to get dehydrated," Ebony agreed.

She unzipped her backpack, pulling out two bottles of water. Jay went to get the snacks out of his, but as soon as he leaned down he let out a yelp and grabbed onto Ebony's arm.

"Snake!" he whispered.

"What?" Ebony cried.

"There, in the bushes," Jay said. "I saw a long tail, with a white tip on the end."

Ebony froze. She knew that if it was a snake the best thing to do was to keep still. Many snakes were venomous but if they didn't feel threatened by any sudden movements they would leave them alone. Jay pointed to the bush. Ebony held her breath and peered down. Jay was right. He had seen something. But it wasn't a snake. It had a furry tail! Very quietly the two Eco

Rangers edged toward the bushes. Ebony gently moved the leaves aside. A small frightened-looking animal stared at her with wide brown eyes.

"Look, it's a possum!" Ebony exclaimed.

"Oh, I knew it wasn't a snake," Jay said, looking relieved.

Ebony laughed. "Maybe you need to clean your glasses better."

It was easy to mistake that long gray-brown tail with the white tip on the end for a reptile. Ebony had sometimes seen possums in the trees in her backyard at home but never on the ground. They were nocturnal, so this one must have been scared from the fire to be out during the day. She looked around. Beside the bushes was a large tree that was blackened and burned. She wondered if it had been the possum's home before the fire.

"Is it okay?" Jay asked. He peered down at the poor possum covered in ash. It was crouched low and chittered quietly.

"I don't know," Ebony admitted. "It must have come down from that tree to save itself from the fire. But look how its feet are blackened. It's been burned from the hot ground."

"We need to get this little one to the wildlife hospital," Jay said.

Ebony agreed. She pulled out a pair of gloves from her backpack and put them on. Possums weren't dangerous, but they did have sharp little claws. She had to be careful to protect her hands.

"You get the carrier ready, and I'll grab the sheet," Ebony said.

Just as they'd been taught at the wildlife hospital, Jay lifted the lid of the carrier, ready. He placed a rolled-up blanket inside, so the possum had something to hold onto in there and would feel safe. Ebony got the sheet and held it across her two open hands. She very slowly stepped toward the little possum. When she was close enough, she gently threw the sheet over it. She grasped the possum firmly but gently by the back of the neck through the sheet with one hand and held onto its tail with the other hand, then placed it carefully in the carrier. Ebony heard the possum scratching for a moment. She put the sheet over the carrier, so it would feel more relaxed in the dark. It settled down quietly then.

"We should mark this spot, so we know where it came from to return it later," Jay added.

Ebony nodded. She pulled the green hairband back out of her hair and passed it to Jay. "That will do!" she said.

He nodded and wrapped it around the stick poking out of the fallen log.

"Let's get the possum back to the wildlife hospital as fast as possible," Ebony said.

Ebony sent a text message to the vet's to let them know they were bringing in an injured animal. Then they made their way back, passing the taped-off area where the firefighters had marked the fire spots. Jay lifted the carrier with the possum inside carefully in his arms while Ebony slung on her backpack. The summer sun rose higher in the sky.

"Let's take a shortcut through the campgrounds," Ebony said.

Non-campers weren't supposed to enter the grounds, but they needed to get the possum to the wildlife hospital urgently. Anyway, the camp was still closed after the fire. There was no one around. They walked across the grassy sites, marked out with numbers painted on posts. The grass was now brown. The concrete slabs for trailers were all vacant. Some were blackened on one side where the fire had been the hottest. The only color was from the firefighter marking tape.

"We'd better check on the possum, it

hasn't moved much in here," Jay said.

Ebony agreed, and Jay put the carrier down. Ebony pulled aside the sheet covering the carrier and peeked in through the breathing holes to check it was okay. The possum held onto the rolled blanket and she could see how sore its paws looked. It stared at her with big brown eyes. She slowly lifted the lid of the carrier and reached in, placing her hand just above where the possum's feet were. She could feel the heat coming off them, especially where they had been burned the worst on its little paw pads.

"Its feet are so hot," Ebony said.

"We need to cool them down," Jay suggested.

He pulled out two water bottles from his bag and untwisted the lid off one of them.

"Good idea," Ebony said.

She wrapped the possum in the sheet, leaving just its head and feet poking out at either end. Jay poured the water slowly over its feet until it was all gone and did the same with the second bottle. Ebony held the possum's paws up under her chin to test them. She could still feel some heat coming from them. She placed the possum back in the carrier.

"We need some more water," Ebony said. She looked around the campgrounds and at the far edge, she could see a shower block and restrooms. The bricks from the building were orange, except where the fire had licked the edges, turning them black.

"We can refill the water bottles over there," she said.

"It looks a little creepy," Jay said, frowning.

"I'll go in there," Ebony said, rolling her eyes. "I'll refill both water bottles and we can cool the possum's feet again. I'll be right back."

She made her way inside the restrooms. The floor in the shower cubicle was wet.

That was strange. It should have been dry inside, especially because the campgrounds had been closed since the fire. She checked the taps. They weren't leaking. She went over to the sink and filled the bottles. As she went to leave, she noticed something pink lying on the end of the bench. She picked up the object and took it with her. Now she was sure of it, someone had been in here since the fire.

"Look what I found in the restrooms," Ebony said.

She showed Jay the pink toothbrush.

"A camper probably left it behind," Jay said, shrugging.

Ebony shoved the toothbrush under his nose.

"Mmm, minty," Jay said.

"Exactly, and it's still damp," Ebony said. "The floor of the showers was wet, too. Someone was in there just before us."

"Why?" Jay asked.

"I don't know, but for now we have to get this possum's paws cooled and get it to the vet's," she said.

Ebony took the possum back out and it started wriggling in her arms and made a little chirruping sound.

The Eco Rangers poured fresh water over the ringtail's feet. This time when Ebony held its paws up under her chin they were much cooler. Jay opened the carrier again and Ebony placed the possum back inside. This time it curled into the blanket and closed its eyes, wrapping its long tail around itself as it fell asleep. Jay closed the lid and picked up the carrier. As Ebony followed Jay toward the track leading back out of the campgrounds, she wondered what someone had been doing here when the grounds were closed.

It was busy by the time the Eco Rangers got to the wildlife hospital. Judy at reception was on the phone, her strawberry-blonde curls bouncing as she took in the new arrivals and calls. "An echidna...? Yes, bring it in. Do you have a bin with a lid you can put it in? They are good at escaping... Great. Don't forget some air holes... Okay, we'll see you then." The moment she put the phone down it rang again. When she spotted the Eco Rangers, she asked the person on the other end of the line to hold.

"Go right through, Eco Rangers," she

said. "The vets are expecting you."

Ebony and Jay, who held the carrier, made their way up the corridor, past the glass walls of the hospital, and to the very end, where the vets were working. Doctor Bat smiled and waved them in when she spotted them. Doctor Tan was at a table. He finished bandaging a kangaroo's burned tail, then the vet nurse took it to the recovery room. Doctor Tan pulled his gloves off his long fingers and tossed them in the bin, coming over to see them.

"Who do we have here?" Doctor Bat said, tucking a loose strand of gray hair behind her ear.

Jay gently placed the carrier down on the bed and the vet peered inside.

"It's a ringtail possum," she cooed.

"We found it under some bushes," Ebony explained. "It's been burned."

Doctor Bat put on her surgical gloves and gently removed the possum from the carrier. It was still clutching the blanket, like it was a teddy bear. The ringtail opened its eyes and stared up at her.

"Heart rate is strong," said the vet, checking the animal. "But this little one's having a bit of trouble breathing. It must have inhaled some smoke due to the wildfire. It seems alert but we'll need to get it some oxygen immediately."

Doctor Tan got the oxygen ready while Doctor Bat removed soot from the possum's eyes and nostrils with a cotton pad. When that was done, Doctor Tan placed the small breathing mask over the possum's face. "That feels better, doesn't it?" he said.

Doctor Bat then felt the possum for injuries but it looked fine. She pinched the possum's fur lightly.

"Hmmm, this female possum is very dehydrated, too. It's lucky you found her when you did, Eco Rangers. She'll need a drip with fluids, please, Doctor Tan."

He nodded and prepared a tube that he attached to a bag of liquid.

"Her feet are burned, too," Ebony said.

"We poured some water over them because they were so hot," Jay added.

Doctor Bat very gently looked at her burned feet while Doctor Tan attached the drip for the possum.

"Hmm, yes, lots of these animals get burned walking on the hot ground. It's a good thing you cooled her feet, that has helped a lot. Now we can put some cream on and bandage her feet up."

"So, she'll be okay?" Ebony asked.

"Yes! After we've treated these burns we'll give her some medicine, so they don't get infected. With the oxygen and fluids, too, she should recover well."

"Then I think we'll call her Mira," Ebony said.

"Mira?" Doctor Tan asked.

"Yes, it's short for miracle," she explained.

"It sure is a miracle you two rescued her," Doctor Tan said.

"She'll need to stay here for a couple of days," Doctor Bat continued. "The longer part will be having to care for her until her paws are fully recovered and there's enough new growth in the bush to return her to her home," Doctor Bat added. "Possums must be returned to their original homes. They don't like to be relocated to a different place."

"Sounds like a job for the Eco Rangers!" Jay said.

"That would be great if you could be our carers for this possum, if it's okay with your parents, of course," Doctor Bat said. "As you can see, we'll have a lot of work to do here for a while yet."

"First, you can help us clean Mira and bandage her feet," Doctor Tan added.

The Eco Rangers helped the vets cool her feet one more time with water, then dried them. The vets put a cream on her feet while Ebony and Jay cut up bandages into small squares that were then taped around her feet. Lastly, they brushed the ash off her fur. Then the vets placed Mira in a possum pouch and put her back in the carrier to sleep.

"Great work!" Doctor Tan said. "You can go now, and we'll look after Mira until she's ready to go home with you."

"It's a good idea to get some bark and leaves from the place where you found her too," Doctor Bat added. "That way, she'll feel like she's at home. She won't be able to walk around for a few days yet, but she'll like having those things around her in her carrier."

Ebony thought of the bushland where they had met Mira and of the wet bathroom and freshly used toothbrush she had found.

"There's one other thing…" she began.

At that moment, a hurt echidna was brought in. *It must be the one Judy was talking about over the phone*, Ebony thought.

"Sorry, Eco Rangers, we've got to help this little one now," Doctor Tan said, wiping his sweaty brow. "We'll call you the day after tomorrow, when it's time to collect Mira."

The Eco Rangers nodded and left the vets to their work. Ebony couldn't help thinking about the wet floor and toothbrush though. They did have a reason to go back to the campsite, to collect foliage for Mira's carrier. It was a chance to do some more investigating. No one was supposed to be camping until the grounds were reopened.

❀

The next day after school, the Eco Rangers set off for the campgrounds again, with a bag to collect some leaves and bark for Mira. Jay's mom had agreed Mira could stay at their house if the Eco Rangers collected everything the possum needed themselves. They retraced their path until they found the same log, still marked with Ebony's green hairband to show where they'd found the possum. Most of the trees were blackened, but there were some parts where the bark was still brown and flaky, with some green leaves. Ebony and Jay picked up some leaves and bark that had fallen to the ground around the trees until the bag was full. Happy they had enough, Jay slung the bag over his back, hunching over like Santa with a bag full of toys. They cut across the campgrounds again. As they walked across the vacant campsite, Ebony thought she heard a rustling in the bushes to one side.

"Did you hear something?" Ebony asked Jay. "Maybe it's another animal."

Jay agreed. "Let's check."

It could be another injured possum, or another land animal like a wallaby or wombat. Even though the bushland had been searched for any animals injured in the wildfire, there could still be sick wildlife that couldn't find food or water after the devastating fire.

"Over there," Jay said, hearing the rustling this time.

The Eco Rangers moved through the bush as quietly as they could, not wanting to scare off a sick or injured animal that might already be stressed. The bush thinned out again further ahead and soon they came to a small clearing. The ground was black, with a scattering of brown leaves, from where the wildfire had been, but Ebony could tell it would have been grassy before the fire struck. She looked around the edges of the clearing, but she couldn't see any animals.

"I can't hear it any more," Jay said.

"Must have just been the breeze rustling the leaves," Ebony said. "We'd better head back home."

She was about to turn back toward the

campgrounds when she noticed something red flash in the bushland.

"There!" she yelled.

Ebony and Jay ran toward it. There it was again. It was no animal. Someone was running away from them. She saw another, smaller figure as well. There were two people. But what were they doing here?

"Hey, come back!" Ebony shouted.

Ebony and Jay ran after the people, but they were too quick and soon disappeared into the bushland.

"That's weird they ran off like that," Jay said.

"Yeah," Ebony agreed. "Maybe they're just shy of strangers. At least it wasn't an injured animal. We'd better get this bark back home. It's getting late, and we've got school tomorrow."

They went back in the direction they'd come, but as they trod through the clearing,

Ebony noticed a dark patch to their left. She hadn't seen it before because they were too busy trying to find out where the noise they'd heard had come from. She went over.

"What now?" Jay said, rolling his eyes behind his glasses at his friend in a knowing way. She was always finding something to investigate!

Ebony stopped at the spot. It was an old campfire. Gray stones were placed in a circle and they were charred black. There were coals and ashes in the middle from a fire that had burned out. Ebony touched the ground. When she looked at her hand it was covered in a gray clay-like powder. She wondered who had built the fire. Could it be the same people who had just run away from her? But why were they hiding when the grounds were closed for campers? She thought back to the wet shower cubicle in the restrooms. It must have been those people, and that proved they must be staying around here, somewhere.

"We have to find out who those people are, and why they're still staying in the campgrounds when they're closed," Ebony said. Jay nodded and the Eco Rangers made their way back home.

The vets from the wildlife hospital rang the Eco Rangers two days later to say it was time to take Mira home to care for her until she was well enough to return to the wild. When Ebony and Jay arrived after school, Judy waved them straight through to the hospital rooms. Even though they were busy treating other animals needing help after the wildfire, the vets always had time for the Eco Rangers.

"Your possum is doing very well, thanks to you finding her when you did," Doctor Bat said, smiling.

The vet brought out Mira, and Doctor

Tan put on a pair of rubber gloves. Jay held the possum while the vet changed her bandages. When he'd finished, he stripped off his gloves and smiled.

"Mira is a good healer. She is ready to go home with you," he said. "You can keep her in this bigger carrier for a few more days, while her feet are still bandaged. Once the bandages are off for good, you'll be able to release her into an enclosure."

Doctor Bat put Mira in a special pouch. She looked happy to be in the cloth sleeping bag, with just her little head poking out. She then placed her inside the bigger carrier and covered it with a sheet to keep her cozy.

Doctor Tan handed the Eco Rangers a bag of food. "This is a mix of her natural food. Blossoms, shoots, leaves. It's sweetened a little to get her energy back up. You can put a spoonful of this in her food bowl each evening, and fresh water."

"Eww... I'm glad I'm not a possum.

Too much green food for me," Jay said, peering into the bag.

Doctor Bat laughed.

"Here is a list of fruit and vegetables Mira can eat as well," Doctor Tan said, explaining how to look after the ringtail. "Oh, and you'll need to bring her to the hospital a few times a week, so we can change her bandages. If there are any problems, or you're worried about her, you know where to find us."

That evening, the Eco Rangers brought Mira to Jay's house. He had the perfect nook in the living room to keep her cozy. When her feet were healed, his family's old chicken coop in the backyard would make the perfect enclosure. Ebony kept her in the little pouch and held her like a baby while Jay offered her teaspoons of water. She lapped it up, her little round ears and whiskers twitching. Ebony laughed at her soft pink nose, now wet and moist. Then she offered her some small pieces of fruit, holding them out to her. Mira nibbled on them happily. When she was done, Jay returned her to the carrier, keeping her in the small dark space while she settled in. The Eco Rangers had lined it with leaves and bark they'd collected, and she had a small blanket in one corner where they placed the pouch. Possums liked to be kept warm and snug.

"I think she'll be okay in there tonight," Ebony said, placing the sheet over the carrier to help her feel calm and relaxed so she could fall sleep.

"Let's get something to eat," Jay agreed, rubbing his belly.

Ebony forgot they hadn't eaten anything. They'd gone straight from school to collect Mira. They went into the kitchen and made some peanut butter sandwiches. Jay's mom

came in to check on them.

"How's our little rescue possum feeling?" she asked.

"She's doing really well," Jay said, leading his mom into the living room.

"You can have a look at her," Ebony added, pulling the sheet that was covering Mira's carrier aside gently.

Jay's mom looked inside. "She is very cute," she said, smiling. Then she looked at her bandaged feet. "I hope those feet heal up well."

Jay explained the bandages would be taken off once the vets were happy her feet were healed enough.

"Can we use the old chicken coop when Mira is better?" Jay suggested. "She'll need to get used to walking around again until she can be released."

"I don't see why not," Jay's mom agreed.

The two Eco Rangers cheered. Looking after Mira was going to be so much fun!

On Friday, Jay's mom and dad helped them get Mira's temporary enclosure ready for her to live in until she could be returned to her home in the bush. Ebony's mom came over as well, bringing some old dishes to use for food and water. The possum needed to be better, but so did her bush home before she could go back. Jay's dad dragged over some branches that had fallen in their yard.

"How are these for the ringtail to climb on?" he asked.

"They're great, Dad," Jay said.

Jay set about placing the branches while Ebony put the dishes her mom gave her in one corner. There was one for water and another for the food mix the vets had given them.

Next, they put in some leaves and bits of bark. When they were just about finished, Ebony looked around.

"There's something missing, but I'm not sure what," she said.

At that moment, Jay's mom came out. She was carrying something in her hands.

"This?" she asked. "I read ringtails like to have a little nesting spot they can sleep in, so I made this from an old plant basket I had lying around."

Ebony squealed in delight and they hung the basket from the side of the enclosure for Mira to sleep in.

Now the enclosure was just right. If the vets removed Mira's bandages for good after the weekend, she would be able to make the enclosure her new temporary home.

"How about some well-deserved burgers and fries for dinner?" Jay's dad suggested. He turned to Ebony's mom. "Would you and Ebony like to join us?"

"We'd love to!" Ebony cried.

"Ebony!" her mom laughed. "That would be lovely, thank-you."

Jay's dad took the order for burgers and fries, while his mom went inside to organize the table for the guests. Meanwhile, the two kids tended to Mira. As the sun went down Mira uncurled her tail, and her big brown eyes opened.

"I think Mira's ready for dinner, too," Jay grinned.

"It looks like it," Ebony agreed, while putting on her gloves, then she took Mira out of the carrier. She stroked the top of her soft gray head between her little, pink rounded ears. She liked being patted and she pushed against Ebony's hand wanting more. Then Jay came over with the water and held a teaspoonful out to her. She leaned forward toward it and lapped up the water.

Ebony laughed. "She likes that."

Ebony poured some of the food mix from the vets into a small bowl. Mira went over to it, sniffed at the bowl, and started to nibble on it happily. Ebony put her back in her carrier once she was done.

"I bet you'll be happy when those bandages come off forever," Ebony said.

"Dinner time!" Jay's dad called.

Jay closed the lid on the carrier and placed the sheet over it again. He and Ebony washed their hands then they raced to the dinner table.

"It's so nice to sit down all together and share a meal after our hard work," Ebony's mom said.

Everyone nodded. Jay's belly growled, agreeing too, while Ebony took the burgers and fries out of the bag.

"How's little Mira?" Ebony's mom asked as they all filled their plates with food.

"She's eating and drinking lots, so she must be okay," Jay laughed.

"That's great," Ebony's mom said. "It's so sad for the wildlife when they lose their homes to wildfires."

"Yes," Jay's mom agreed. "And worse when they are injured in it."

"At least little Mira will be well looked after here," Jay's dad added.

"How do wildfires start?" Ebony asked.

"Sometimes wildfires are deliberately lit, but mostly when humans cause wildfires it's from someone being careless, or not knowing how to look after nature," Jay's dad said.

"Or, they can be accidental, from an electrical fault," Jay's mom added.

"Even lightning strikes can cause wildfires," Ebony's mom agreed.

Ebony wondered what had caused the wildfires near the campgrounds. *Was it accidental, or did someone cause the fire?* She thought back to the two people she had seen running away, the pink toothbrush she had found in the restroom area even though the campgrounds were closed, and the campfire. The Eco Rangers needed to find out what had really happened, and what those people were doing hanging around the grounds. Ebony looked at Jay. She knew he was thinking the same thing. He never usually chewed over his food so thoughtfully!

The next day the Eco Rangers were ready to set out to the campgrounds early. They needed to get some more fresh leaves and bark for Mira's enclosure, but mostly they wanted to find out who was hiding out at the campsite and why. They packed some snacks, water, Ebony's phone, a compass so they could find their way if they got lost, and a blanket in case they came across any animals. Ebony also added a notepad and pen to record anything else they found, like proper detectives! Before leaving, they changed Mira's water, keeping quiet as she lay sleeping in her pouch. Then they told their parents they'd be back in the afternoon to look after Mira and get her to the wildlife hospital so the vets could change her bandages and check if she was getting better.

Ebony and Jay dropped their bikes at the edge of the campgrounds, hiding them in some nearby bushes. They made their way into the grounds. Ebony was surprised there was new growth starting to appear on the burned trees already. Bright green shoots stood out against the black.

They looked around the campsite and the restroom area. There was no sign of anyone being here this morning. They kept going, until they reached the area where little Mira had been found in the first place.

"There are lots of leaves and bark over there for Mira," Ebony said, pointing to a nearby bushy area.

The Eco Rangers walked through the scrub and started collecting some foliage they thought Mira would like.

They searched the bushes, picking up some more leaves. Just as they were leaving, Ebony spied a rocky crevice.

"Let's go over there," she said.

Jay nodded. They made their way toward the rocks. They climbed over boulders and smaller rocks to get to the larger outcrop. Ebony reached it first. Jay followed behind, puffing. There were several huge rocks that leaned against each other, making a cave. Ebony bent down and peered inside. She gasped.

"What is it?" Jay said.

He looked in as well. There were two camp mattresses laid out side by side, one smaller and one larger. Some empty chip packets and a backpack sat in one corner. A torch, matches, and some newspaper were lying on top of one of the mattresses.

"Wow! There really are two people hiding out here!" Jay said.

"Yeah, and we've just found their camp," Ebony agreed.

"Why would anyone want to camp out here? It would give me the creeps." Jay shivered.

Ebony thought of the campfire, the restroom area where she'd found the toothbrush, and the figures in the bush, who had run away from them. It didn't make any sense. "Why are people hiding out here?" she said.

"And where are they?" Jay asked.

"We have to find them," Ebony replied.

She glanced around. Whoever they were,

they were very good at hiding. There was no sign of them.

"They shouldn't be camping out in the bush alone, especially when the grounds are closed."

Jay felt around in his backpack and pulled out the snacks they had packed, and the water bottles.

"You're thinking about food?" Ebony gasped.

"No, I have an idea," Jay replied. "What if we leave them a note with snacks?"

Ebony nodded with a big grin on her face and pulled out her notepad and pen. She wrote on it: *Enjoy the snacks. Who are you and why are you hiding out here? Are you okay? Your friends, the Eco Rangers.*

The Eco Rangers left their snacks and water bottles at the opening of the rock cave. Ebony put the note next to it and left her pen, holding the paper down. Then they made their way back out of the campgrounds to their bikes. It was time for the Eco Rangers to go home. Mira was waiting for them.

5

Ebony and Jay spent Sunday with the vets in the bushland to help the wildlife after the devastating wildfire by putting out bowls of water for thirsty animals.

As they followed the bush track, Jay put down the first bowl in their stack and Ebony poured in some water. Then they added a few sticks and stones on one side like they'd been shown, so smaller animals wouldn't get stuck inside the bowl if they came to drink from it.

"Look!" Ebony cried.

As soon as they had left the first bowl

a cockatoo flew down and perched on the edge of the bowl. It bent its head down, enjoying the cool water. Jay laughed as the bird lifted its head again, its feathers now sticking together. The bird bobbed its head like it was thanking them.

"It likes it!" Jay said.

"Come on, let's put out some more," Ebony said, smiling.

The Eco Rangers carried on until they had no water left. Though some trees were showing the new growth, the earth was still parched. Seeing the cockatoo come for the water showed how much the animals still needed their help.

Once they were finished, they walked to the start point to meet up with the vets and other volunteers to check everyone was back. Ebony was glad they could help out, but now it was time to get back to Mira. She'd be waking up for her meal soon.

When they got back to Jay's house, Mira

was just waking up and wriggled in her little pouch. Ebony took her out to give her fresh water and pieces of fruit, while Jay added some fresh leaves and bark. Ebony held out a piece of nectarine. Mira sniffed at it and then ate from her hand. Her little whiskers tickled Ebony's fingers as she nibbled down to the end of the fruit. The Eco Rangers giggled. Mira pushed her nose forward, nudging Ebony for some more.

Jay laughed, handing Ebony another piece of fruit for the hungry possum. Once Mira had finished nibbling, Ebony let out a huge yawn.

"I think it's time for the Eco Rangers to go to bed now," Ebony said to Mira.

They returned the possum to her cozy home in the carrier and put the sheet over the top.

"See you tomorrow," Ebony said to Jay, yawning again, as she walked home.

The next afternoon, Jay's mom sat in the hospital waiting area while the Eco Rangers took Mira to the back room. Ebony was excited they'd be able to release Mira into her enclosure if her feet were better. The vets were happy to see how well the little ringtail possum was doing.

Doctor Bat prepared a table with a clean sheet and small scissors for removing Mira's bandages. Doctor Tan gently lifted the possum out of the carrier and took her out of the pouch. Her long tail had been curled up around her while she'd been sleeping, and it slowly stretched out as she woke up on the cold table.

"Sorry to wake you, little one, but you'll feel much better once these bandages are off you," he said, placing her down on the table.

Doctor Bat took out the scissors and snipped the bandages off. She gently wiped the possum's tiny claws and padded feet with a cotton swab. She looked at each paw carefully and smiled.

"They've healed very well. It's time to get this little one into her enclosure while she builds up her strength and fully recovers."

"The bush is starting to grow back near her old home, too," Ebony said.

"That's good news," Doctor Tan said.

"We'll leave you to settle her into her enclosure now," Doctor Bat said. "Let's check her again in a few days to see if she's ready to go back home."

The vets said goodbye to the Eco Rangers and they went back out to where Jay's mom was waiting. She looked away from the television screen when she saw them appear.

"How's Mira?" she asked.

"She's ready to go into her enclosure!" Ebony smiled.

Back at Jay's, the Eco Rangers took Mira out to her new enclosure. Ebony gently put her on the ground while Jay filled up her food and water bowls. Mira looked around, her whiskers shaking. She sniffed the air and then started scampering around her new home. She found her food and water quickly.

"You know what's important, don't you?" Jay said to the possum.

Ebony laughed as Mira sniffed at her water bowl. She leaned in and lapped up some water. Then she moved to the food bowl. She seemed to enjoy it so much she grabbed the edge of the bowl with one front foot, wrapping her tiny claws around it. Her long whiskers trembled as she ate. Then she scampered around, going through the leaf litter they'd left on the ground. After a while she climbed around the enclosure, moving quickly from branch to branch and along the wire edges, using her front and back claws to grasp on. Eventually, she found a flat branch to sit on, and wrapped her tail around to hang on, her body shaking slightly, and she looked all around her. Ebony reached out and patted her on her back. Her fur was so soft. She seemed to sit there happily.

"She likes that," Ebony said.

Jay reached out and stroked her head. When he stopped, she pushed her nose forward.

"She wants more," he laughed, giving her another pat.

She seems excited to be in her new home where she can explore, Ebony thought. Mira was eating well, which was also good. That reminded her, they had to check if the two mysterious hideaways had eaten the food they'd left back at the campgrounds.

On Tuesday after school, Ebony and Jay loaded up their backpacks with their usual supplies, as well as a few ham and cheese sandwiches, juice, fruit, and snacks in case the hideaways came out of hiding and needed more food. They biked to the campgrounds and made their way along the track toward the rock cave. They went to the front of it, where they'd left the food, water and note.

"Look!" Ebony said.

She pointed to the place. The food and water were gone. In their place was a rock.

A scrap of paper was poking out from underneath it. Ebony edged toward it. She moved the rock aside and took the piece of paper. It had her handwriting on it. But when she turned it over, she saw there was fresh writing on the other side.

"They've written back to us!" Ebony exclaimed.

"What does it say?" Jay asked.

Thanks for the food and water. We were very hungry and thirsty. Your new friends, Max and Hilda. PS. Please can you bring some more? Thank-you!

While she was reading it, Jay tapped her on the shoulder. He was pointing toward the rock cave. Ebony leaned forward. Two people were walking toward them. The taller one at the front was a boy. He looked like a teenager and he was wearing a bright red sweater. It was the first person they'd seen the other day. It must be Max. The other one was a girl. She had long blonde braids and was shorter. She seemed a bit younger, she looked about nine or ten. This had to be Hilda. She was the first one to see the Eco Rangers. She smiled and lunged toward them. The older boy grasped her by the arm before she could get to them though and shook his head. The girl frowned. Max looked left and right, then walked toward the Eco Rangers slowly.

"Are you the ones who left us the food? Do you have any more?" the girl said boldly, running out in front of him.

"Hilda! That's not polite," the boy said.

"But I'm still hungry, Max."

"It's okay," Ebony said. "We're the Eco Rangers. I'm Ebony and this is Jay, and you must be Hilda and Max?"

The girl nodded.

"And we brought more food," Jay said.

He unzipped his backpack and pulled out the food. There was plenty for everyone. Ebony laid out the blanket and set out the food, making four places for afternoon tea! The Eco Rangers unwrapped their sandwiches and started to eat. Without saying another word, Max nodded at Hilda and the two sat down in front of their food. They unwrapped the sandwiches and gobbled them up faster than Ebony had ever seen Jay eat! Then they opened the juice bottles and drank it all down. They also had some fruit and cookies, and finally looked full. *They really must have been hungry and thirsty!* Ebony thought. She wasn't sure what to say to them, she didn't want to scare them off again. She was about to ask them something easy, like how old they were, when Jay got in first.

"What are you two doing out here?" Jay asked.

Ebony stretched out her foot and pushed him in the leg. So much for not scaring them off!

"What? Aren't you wondering?" Jay said.

"Yes, but you don't just come and blurt it out like that," Ebony argued.

Hilda giggled. "Are you brother and sister like me and Max? You sound just like us."

"No." Ebony smiled. "We are best friends though."

"We were on an Explorer camping trip," said Max, "and we were busy climbing around these rocks when we realized we'd been separated from our group…'

"You mean we got lost, didn't we?" Hilda interrupted.

"Okay, we got lost. It started to get dark really quickly so we set up a camp…'

"And I got cold," Hilda said.

"Yes, Hilda was freezing so we made a fire. Then we found this cave and we set up camp inside it. Before we knew it, everything was on fire," Max said.

"It was so scary," Hilda added.

"And you've been here ever since?" Ebony asked. "What about your Explorer group?"

"Now who's blurting things out?" Jay said.

Ebony shrugged.

"We're okay here," Max said.

"You can't camp out here on your own!" Jay said.

"I'm thirteen years old. That's old enough," Max said.

"And I'm nine," Hilda said proudly.

"But the campgrounds are closed because of the wildfire," Ebony argued.

"We can't go home—" Hilda began.

"What she means is, we don't want to go just yet, and you can't tell anyone we're here," Max said.

At that moment, Hilda burst into tears. Ebony felt bad she'd asked about it.

"It's okay, we won't say anything," Ebony said. That made her think of something. "Hey, I think I have something of yours, Hilda."

Ebony reached into her bag and Hilda wiped her eyes with the back of her hand, looking over curiously. Ebony pulled out the pink toothbrush! Hilda smiled and took it from Ebony's hand.

"I think you left this behind at the camp restrooms," Ebony said.

"So, you knew we were here days ago?" Max said. "We thought the cleaners took it or something."

"We didn't know for sure, but we thought someone had to have been here or we couldn't have found a freshly used toothbrush," Jay explained.

"And a wet floor after a fire," Ebony added.

"Is that what the Eco Rangers are? Are you real spies?" Hilda asked.

"No," Jay laughed. "We help wildlife."

That reminded Ebony. "Mira!" It must nearly be time to feed her. She pulled out her cell phone and checked.

"Hey! You just said you wouldn't tell anyone," Max cried. He faced Hilda angrily. "See, I told you we couldn't trust them?"

Ebony turned bright red. "I was just checking the time. We have to go, it's time to feed Mira."

"Who's Mira? Is she camping out here, too?" Hilda asked.

"No." Ebony laughed. "She's a ringtail possum. She was caught up in the wildfire. We're looking after her until she is all better."

Hilda and Max looked at each other. Ebony thought they looked a little guilty. Maybe they were just surprised to hear about kids caring for wildlife.

Ebony and Jay left them plenty of food for the next few days, collected the food trash, put it in the backpack, and rolled up the blanket. They said goodbye and promised to be back soon with even more food.

When they got home, Mira was already awake and climbing around. The moment Ebony opened the enclosure door she stopped. She sat still, her long tail wrapped around a branch, and sniffed at the air.

"Are you hungry?" Ebony asked.

Jay gave her some fresh water and food mix in her bowls. Mira sniffed the air again then uncurled her tail and came down the branch, scampering across the ground. She nibbled her food and lapped from her water bowl before returning to her perch up on the branch, her tiny claws helping her climb quickly and easily.

"She's getting faster on those paws," Jay said.

Ebony had pieces of apple in her shirt pocket for the possum. She took some out and held them toward her. Mira scrambled forward and took the pieces from Ebony's hand, holding them in her claws and nibbling at them. When Ebony reached into her pocket for more, Mira leaped across from the branch onto Ebony's shoulder. She crawled down and reached into her pocket, taking out a piece of apple.

"You cheeky girl," Ebony said.

Jay laughed. "She's clever!"

Mira ate the rest of the apple and then crawled into Ebony's pocket again, settling in there.

"I think she's made your pocket her new pouch," Jay laughed.

After two more days caring for Mira, it was time to take her for her final checkup at the wildlife hospital. This time the Eco Rangers didn't need the carrier. The ringtail possum had become used to traveling around in Ebony's shirt pocket and she was happy to sleep there. Sometimes she would poke her little head out to see what was going on around her, and she would even climb onto Ebony's shoulder while Jay hand-fed her pieces of fruit.

The vets smiled when they saw the Eco

Rangers with their new friend.

"It looks like you've been taking very good care of Mira." Doctor Bat smiled. "Let's check her over to see if she's ready to go back home."

Ebony took Mira from her pocket and Doctor Bat checked her paws, her heart rate, her breathing, fur, and eyes.

"Excellent job, Eco Rangers. She'll be ready for a soft release now."

"What does that mean?" Jay asked.

"She has become used to you, so she might not be quite ready to stay out in the bush without you," Doctor Tan explained. "That means you can release her back to her home but come back and check on her and give her some extra food each day until she's happy to be left on her own again."

The Eco Rangers smiled. It would be good not having to say goodbye forever just yet!

Doctor Bat gave Mira back to Ebony.

She quickly scurried up her arm, onto her shoulder, and down into her shirt pocket where some fruit pieces were waiting for her to nibble on after her checkup.

"How's her bush home? Is it green enough now?" Doctor Tan asked.

"Yes," Ebony said. "We were there just yesterday."

"When we took some food for…" Jay began.

Ebony nudged him. They'd promised they wouldn't tell anyone about Hilda and Max.

"Some wildlife," Jay said quickly.

"Okay. Then Mira is ready to return to her own home," Doctor Tan said.

"Thanks, Doctor Tan. Thanks, Doctor Bat," Ebony said.

The Eco Rangers made their way back out of the hospital. When they got to the waiting area, Ebony glanced up at the television screen. She was surprised to see a photo of two familiar faces. She gripped Jay's arm and pointed. They listened in to the news report.

"A nine-year-old girl and her teenage brother are still missing since the wildfire. The alert was raised after they failed to return to their home town almost a week ago, after a camping trip. Search teams are still doing everything they can to locate them."

"That's Hilda and Max!" Ebony exclaimed.

"They're supposed to be home by now," Jay said.

"Yeah, their family must be so worried," Ebony agreed.

"We need to tell them about the news report," Jay said.

"Let's do that straight after we release Mira," Ebony suggested.

7

The next day, Ebony and Jay took Mira back to the campgrounds. They followed the path they'd taken when they first found her until they reached the place where Mira came from. They stopped at the log, still marked with Ebony's hairband. Jay pulled a container out of his backpack. He opened the lid and and took out an apple, holding it toward Mira.

"Here, see?" he said.

Mira climbed out of Ebony's pocket and scurried up to her shoulder. She leaned forward and took the apple from Jay. She held it between her two paws and nibbled on the fruit. It had started to get windy and the branches swayed in the breeze. It was time to get Mira to her tree house. The Eco Rangers stopped at the base of it.

"It's time to go now," Ebony said.

She walked over to a nearby tree and gently placed the possum on a branch, the leaves fluttering in the wind. But Mira scampered back along the branch to the trunk, leaped across it and ran down onto the ground. She scurried in the other direction.

"Hey! Where are you going?" Ebony said, worried.

The Eco Rangers followed the possum. There were pieces of branches lying around and charred bits of wood everywhere.

"Why is she heading that way?" Jay asked.

Mira stopped when she came to another, taller tree. She clawed at the blackened trunk.

"Is this tree your home?" Ebony asked her.

"Hey! Look at this!" Jay said, pointing to a spot higher on the trunk of the tree.

He was gesturing to a long crack down the front of the blackened tree.

"This is from a lightning strike!" he exclaimed. "That's one of the things the firefighters told us to look out for."

"I think we've found what caused the wildfire!" Ebony agreed.

Ebony got out her cell phone and took a photo of the tree to show the fire department. Mira then sniffed the air. At that moment she turned from the tree and ran up to Ebony, racing up to her shoulder again.

"Mira? What's wrong? Don't you want to go home?"

"Maybe she's confused about which is her tree," Jay said.

The little possum wriggled her nose again. Jay copied.

"What are you doing?" Ebony said, laughing at her friend.

"Do you smell something?"

Ebony stood up and sniffed the air, too. It was a little smoky, but maybe she was just imagining it after the wildfires. The wind was howling through the trees by now though and Mira's whiskers shook.

"Look!" Jay pointed through the trees.

Smoke was swirling through them like a mist.

"Oh no, the wind must have sparked a fire. It's getting stronger, too," Ebony said.

She pulled out her cell phone again and called the emergency number. "Fire. Gum Lane Campgrounds. No, just the two of us. Okay. Come quickly, please." She turned to Jay. "They're on their way."

"I hope they hurry," Jay said, pointing to the trees on the opposite side.

"Oh no!" Ebony said, seeing an orange glow. "Come on, we need to get out of here."

Mira crawled into Ebony's pocket as if she understood. The Eco Rangers started running in the opposite direction, toward home. Then Ebony remembered.

"Max and Hilda! They're in the bush up there. We have to warn them," she said.

Ebony and Jay turned and ran toward the rocky outcrop. The smoky smell was getting stronger, but they couldn't leave Max and Hilda out there. The air felt warm and thick, and Ebony found she got puffed quickly. It seemed like ages, but they soon came to the rock cave. She and Jay climbed up the rocks to the entrance. But when they got there, all of Max and Hilda's belongings were gone and they were nowhere to be seen.

"How will we find them?" Ebony cried.

"Maybe they saw the smoke, too, and are already out of the campgrounds," Jay said.

Ebony looked past the rocky outcrop. She could see three small orange glows scattered in the bush. Fire. The wind must have made the hot spots from the wildfire start up again in the dry bush.

"Let's climb to the top and see if we can spot them from there," Ebony suggested.

Jay was already climbing up onto the top of the rocky outcrop and Ebony scrambled up behind him. From up high they could see exactly where the spot fires had started, making a triangle shape. They needed to find Max and Hilda before they joined up or they could get cut off by wildfire. But the bush was dense, and Ebony couldn't see anyone. She was about to climb back down when she saw movement in the bushland.

"There!" she said, pointing.

Jay squinted his eyes, but it was just a group of wallabies moving through the bush. Animals could sense the danger early and they were hopping away from the burning scrub. The wind pushed Ebony's hair around her face. It was getting stronger.

That wasn't good for fires.

"I hope Max and Hilda aren't out there somewhere," Ebony said.

"What if we call out to them?" Jay said. He placed his hands in a cup around his mouth and called out their names, hoping they would hear him. "Max! Hilda!"

The sound of Jay's voice echoed out to the bush. Then the Eco Rangers listened, but it was still and quiet. Even the birds were silent.

"Try it again!" Ebony said.

Jay cupped his hands to his mouth again. "Max! Hilda!"

This time Ebony thought she heard something. It was faint, but someone was sending a signal back to them. She looked toward the sound and she could see two figures in the distance. They were right in the middle of the triangle of spot fires. The Eco Rangers had to get to them before the fires joined up. As if knowing,

Mira scampered up to Ebony's shoulder and twittered in her ear. Ebony gave her a pat on the head, Mira shook her whiskers and returned to Ebony's shirt pocket. The ringtail knew the danger, too.

Jay called back again to Max and Hilda, telling them they were coming. Then the Eco Rangers raced back down the hill, slipping and sliding as they went. Down at the bottom, Ebony and Jay ran toward Max and Hilda, through the bushes that scratched at their arms and legs as they went. The smoke was getting thicker, and it was harder to see where they were going. Jay kept calling and the sound of Max's return cries got louder. At least they were heading in the right direction. As they got closer, Ebony could hear someone coughing. It sounded like little Hilda. They kept moving and Ebony could see the glow of the fire as it moved in closer. She worried they wouldn't make it to them in time.

Just as Ebony thought she couldn't run any further, they nearly crashed straight into Max and Hilda, stumbling in the opposite direction toward them, their packs on their backs making them look like two turtles. Hilda's face was dirty and streaked with tears. She was coughing as she wrapped her arms around Ebony.

"It's okay," Ebony said. "We've found you now."

"I was so scared," Hilda said.

Ebony and Jay looked to Max, whose eyes were wide with fear.

"Come on, that fire's spreading fast. We need to get to a safe place," Jay said.

"There's nowhere for us to go," Max argued.

"It's okay, I've called emergency. They'll be here soon but we've got to keep clear of the path of the fire," Ebony said.

"You called what?" Max said, his face turning pale.

"We need help. Fires can spread fast," Ebony explained.

Hilda and Max looked at each other fearfully.

"No one can find us out here," Max said. "We'll wait it out in the cave. We'll be safe in there."

"Not if the fire goes through," Jay said.

"You have to come with us," Ebony said.

She stretched out her hand to Hilda but just as she was about to take it, Max stopped her.

"We can't go with you!" Max said.

She thought back to the news report. Why hadn't Max and Hilda gone home? She remembered the campfire they'd found. Did they think they had caused the wildfire? Is that why they were hiding out? There was no time to talk about it now.

"It will be okay, I promise," Ebony said. "We have to get to a safe place first."

Ebony could now see flames coming up

from the bushland. The triangle of fire was joining. They had to move quickly. But Max stood there, shaking his head.

At that moment, Mira climbed out of Ebony's pocket. Hilda screamed.

Ebony looked at the possum, sitting on her shoulder.

"This is Mira. She's the ringtail possum we are looking after." That gave Ebony an idea. "We need to get her away from the smoke. We need you to come with us, so we can help her."

Hilda looked at Max pleadingly.

Max sighed. "Okay, where to?"

"We can go to the side of it, to the restroom block," Jay said.

Ebony nodded. It was the best plan and hopefully they would be safe there until help came. At that moment, there was a crashing sound and a slow crackle. The fire was moving quickly in their direction.

"Let's go!" Jay yelled.

The four of them ran as fast as they could, toward the campground restroom area. But the smoke became so thick that they couldn't see where they were going any more. Soon they found themselves off the bush track and the wildfire was spreading fast.

8

"Which way is it?" Max said.

"I think the campgrounds are over here," Jay replied.

"No, they're this way," Ebony said.

Hilda coughed hard. The smoke was making it difficult for all of them to breathe. Ebony had an idea. She reached into her backpack and pulled out her compass. She held it up.

"The campgrounds are to the north," she said. She looked at the red arrow and turned until they were facing the right direction. "This way."

Max and Hilda started to walk in that direction.

"Wait! The smoke is too thick, and the air is heating up. We need to protect ourselves from the fire first," said Jay.

Living near the bush, Ebony and Jay had learned what to do in case of a wildfire. Jay quickly instructed Max and Hilda to put on their pants and long-sleeved tops.

"But won't that make us hotter?" Max asked.

"It'll protect your skin," Jay explained.

They took their backpacks off and did what the Eco Rangers said. Ebony got out the drink bottles and asked them to pass over any small pieces of clothing they had in their bags.

Jay wetted down two T-shirts and pieces of underwear with the water from the drink bottles.

"Put them over your mouths," he said, handing Max and Hilda a piece of their underwear each.

"No way!" Max said.

"It'll keep the smoke out," Jay explained.

Max and Hilda put their underwear over their faces like a mask.

"No one is to ever find out I put underwear on my head," Max groaned.

Ebony and Jay smiled, coughing. Then they held a T-shirt over each of their own mouths.

Hilda was finding it hardest being the smallest. Jay pulled out the woolen blanket they used for wildlife rescues and handed it to her.

"Put this around your shoulders. It will help protect you."

Hilda nodded and did as he said. Tears filled her eyes.

"Look, now you're our superhero with a fire blanket cape protecting you," Ebony said.

That made her smile, and Ebony held

out the compass, heading north through the haze.

Ebony could feel the heat rising as they raced away from the wildfire, heading north. The bushland was thick but soon she saw a cleared patch. They had found the bush path again. The Eco Rangers led Max and Hilda toward it and they stumbled along the stony track. Ebony looked over her shoulder. The fire was getting bigger, and closer. They had to hurry.

"There, up ahead!" Jay yelled.

He was right. Jay had found the campgrounds. Ebony led the way to the right, toward the restroom. It would be safest there until help could arrive. They ran toward it, so close now, and Ebony led them all inside the women's restrooms.

"No one is to tell anyone I was in the girls' restrooms when we get out of here," Jay said.

That made Hilda giggle. Jay pulled the thick metal door closed behind them.

Ebony raced to the taps first and wetted down all their clothing face masks, handing them back out again. Then she grabbed another T-shirt, rolled it up, and put it in the gap at the bottom of the door. When they'd done all that they huddled in the farthest corner. Hilda started to cough again from all the smoke. Ebony was worried it was getting worse. They had to keep as low as they could, away from the smoke, so she got Hilda to crouch down under her blanket. Hilda started to sob. Max tried to soothe her, but nothing worked. She was frightened.

"Do we have any more fruit?" Jay asked.

"Not still thinking of food, are you?" Ebony cried.

"No, I have an idea."

Ebony frowned and handed Jay the fruit she had for Mira. Jay took a piece and gave it to Hilda.

"Here, hold this toward Ebony's pocket," he said to her.

Ebony got it now. She leaned forward. Mira poked her little furry head out. Then she crawled out and leaned toward Hilda.

"Won't she bite?" Max said.

"Only the fruit," Jay said. "Try it, Hilda."

Hilda held it out to Mira. She scampered down and took the fruit gently from Hilda's hand. She started nibbling on it.

"She's so cute," Hilda said.

"Mira loves being patted, too," Ebony suggested.

Hilda slowly reached out and stroked Mira on the head. The possum nuzzled her.

"She's soft," Hilda said, smiling.

Everyone had forgotten all about the danger they were in for a moment and Hilda wasn't coughing so badly.

"She sure is cute," Max said. "Why don't you have her as your pet?"

"It would be nice to keep her, but she belongs in the bush," Ebony said.

Hilda and Max nodded knowingly. Ebony realized they must be missing their home by now, too.

"We were taking Mira back to her tree when she smelled the smoke," Jay added. Max and Hilda looked at each other with that guilty look, and Hilda's eyes filled with tears again.

"It's okay," Ebony said, trying to help her feel better. "The fire department will be here soon, and we'll all be okay."

"It's not that…" she said and started to sob harder now.

"It's our fault this poor little possum got hurt," Max continued.

Ebony and Jay frowned at each other. How could it be their fault?

"We started the wildfire," Hilda cried, and a new flood of tears began.

"We didn't mean it," Max explained.

"We built a campfire. Then we went back to the cave to get the marshmallows to toast over it when we heard a huge explosion. When we turned back around, the fire had already started."

"Is that why you're hiding out?"

"We couldn't go back home. We'd be in so much trouble."

"But you didn't start the wildfire," Jay said.

"What do you mean?"

"It wasn't the campfire that made that sound," Ebony said, "It was a lightning strike. It hit a tree and caused the fire."

"Are you sure?" Max asked.

"Yes," Ebony said. "Jay found the tree the lightning struck."

"Mira did actually," Jay corrected.

Ebony showed Max and Hilda the photo of the tree.

"See? This big crack down the middle means it's been hit by lightning."

Max and Hilda looked at each other.

"It wasn't our fault?" Max said, smiling for the first time.

"No!" Ebony said.

"We can go home then?" Hilda asked, wiping away her tears.

"Um, not just yet," Ebony said.

Ebony looked to the closed restroom area door. She knew now how the animals must feel when they get trapped in a wildfire.

9

The Eco Rangers, Max, Hilda, and Mira stayed huddled in the restroom area. Ebony could feel it getting hotter inside and smoke started to come in through the gaps. Hilda's coughing from the smoke got worse. They were all coughing a bit now. The clothing covering their faces had all dried out, so they wetted them down again. Then Ebony wetted the rolled-up T-shirt under the doorway crack again, as it had dried out completely. She hoped the fire department would be here soon, and that they would be found, hiding in here.

At that moment, Ebony heard a siren. They all looked at each other hopefully. Had help arrived? But how would anyone know they were in here? Ebony went over to the restroom area door. She held her hand up, but she could feel the heat coming off it. It wasn't safe to open it. She knew never to open a hot door if there was a fire because the fire could quickly move inside. The sound grew louder. Then stopped. She looked at her phone. There was no service any more. They all started yelling for help as loud as they could, but Ebony didn't know if anyone could hear them through the thick brick walls and solid metal door. Then Mira crawled out of Ebony's pocket and scrambled down her arm and leaped to the floor.

"Mira!" Ebony cried.

She tried to catch her but Mira was too fast for Ebony. The ringtail raced into one of the shower cubicles. Ebony chased after her, but Mira disappeared through a drain hole in the corner of the shower, leading outside.

"Oh no! She'll get hurt!"

For a few awful minutes, Ebony looked for Mira, wishing she would come back safely. Ebony crouched down at the hole and yelled out to Mira until her voice was almost gone. She sat back helplessly, wishing she'd held on to the possum and imagining what could happen to her out there. She'd almost forgotten that they needed rescuing, too. Then she heard something...

"Hello?" came a voice from outside.

That was weird. An eye appeared through a hole in the wall of the restroom area. Ebony leaped back in fright.

"Is anyone in there? This is Firefighter Dan Muller. Hello?"

"We're in here!" Jay yelled.

Max, Hilda and then Ebony all joined in, shouting that they were inside.

Ebony heard him yell to someone outside. "Hey, it sounds like there are kids inside the shower block." Then he came back to the hole. "Is everyone okay in there?"

"Yes, just a bit smoky in here," Jay said, coughing.

"OK. Just hold tight. The firefighters have the blaze under control. We just need to get these smoke levels down. Can you do one thing for me?"

"Sure," Jay said.

"Just keep back from the restroom door. It's super hot right now. We'll have to come in through the top to get you out."

"You got it," Jay agreed.

"Oh, and one more thing. You're lucky this little ringtail possum was around. It came right up to us and led us to you."

"That's Mira. Is she all right?" Ebony yelled from inside.

"She's fine," he said. "And I must be

talking to the Eco Rangers, am I?"

"Yes." Ebony grinned. Nearly everyone knew about the kids who looked after wildlife.

"There are two more of us," Jay said.

"Two more Eco Rangers?" he asked.

"Well, not exactly—."

Max and Hilda looked at him, and shook their heads. "They're our helpers," Jay added.

"Okay, I'll be right back," Dan said.

It felt like a long time waiting for Dan to come back. Smoke was still coming in and Hilda's coughing got worse. Soon she was wheezing, and she had trouble breathing normally.

"Do you think they'll take long?" Max asked.

"I'm sure they'll be as quick as they can," Ebony said, starting to feel out of breath, too.

She really hoped what she said was right. Hilda was looking pale and her chest was moving up and down fast now. Ebony wetted down the cloth again and gave it to Hilda to hold over her face. Nothing seemed to be working now though.

Just as Ebony started coughing too, there was a thumping sound coming from the roof of the restroom area.

"It's them!" Jay said.

Ebony looked up. The tiles on top of the roof were moving. Then a man wearing a breathing mask peered down at them.

"I'm Dan. Is everyone okay?" he asked in a muffled voice.

Ebony looked at Hilda, who was breathing hard. Dan had appeared just in time.

"Hilda's not very well," she said.

"Okay, we'll get Hilda out first," Dan said. "What I'm going to do is lower this rope down. It's got a harness attached. All you need to do is step into it, buckle it up nice and tight, and I'll pull you up, one at a time. Bring just yourselves up, nothing else. Leave any belongings behind."

"Are you ready, Hilda?" Ebony asked.

Hilda shook her head.

"You can do it, I'll help you," Ebony said.

Hilda shook her head again. She was shaking as well now.

"She's afraid of heights," Max called up.

Dan scratched his head. "We don't have much time. The smoke is getting worse. We'll get the rest of you out first. Hilda, you're going to be okay. Give me a thumbs up."

Hilda coughed and held up her shaking thumb. Jay went first after Max insisted he stay with his sister the longest. Jay stepped into the harness and Ebony helped buckle it up for him. Then he gave the signal that he was ready to be lifted. The firefighters pulled him up on the rope and he scrambled onto the roof. The rope was lowered down again, and Ebony went next. She came up safely and Dan handed Mira to her.

"I think this little one is very happy to see you," he said.

Mira crawled along Ebony's arm and settled in her shirt pocket, poking her little head out.

Then it was Max's turn to come up. When he got safely to the top as well, he called down to Hilda, who couldn't stop coughing now.

"It's easy, Hilda. Go on, you can do it. I'm right here waiting for you."

But Hilda shook her head, tears now streaming down her dirty face. Ebony looked around. The fire was much closer than before. The firefighters were fighting it back, spraying water from the hoses onto it, but the smoke was thick around them. They had to get Hilda out fast. Mira crawled out of her shirt pocket up to her shoulder. That gave Ebony an idea. She told Dan and he nodded for her to give it a try.

"Hilda," she said, leaning forward over the gap. "I need some help. Could you hold Mira for me?"

"Me?" Hilda asked, coughing, her eyes lighting up.

"Yes!" Ebony said.

Hilda nodded.

Ebony held Mira in her arms, against her chest, and then leaned forward, releasing her. The possum wriggled her little nose as she gripped onto the rope with her claws and scampered down. Hilda watched as Mira ran down and stopped as she reached the harness.

"Hilda, put your feet next to Mira's paws," said Dan. Hilda looked really frightened but she slowly moved over to the harness and stepped into it.

"Okay, hold on, we're just going

to bring you up a bit."

Mira scampered onto Hilda's arm. Hilda patted the little possum's head. While she was distracted, Dan brought up the rope, bringing Hilda up to safety. She looked around, surprised, when she realized she was out. They still had to get her down off the roof. The firefighters put a ladder against the wall, ready.

"We just need to climb down this ladder now, Hilda, and we'll be back home before you know it."

Hilda was shaking but nodded bravely. The little possum snuggled into Hilda's arms and Dan helped them both down the ladder. They were safe.

Ebony and Jay climbed down the ladder after Hilda. Ebony took Mira from Hilda's arms and she crawled back into Ebony's shirt pocket where she fell asleep, just like she knew her work was done. Ebony looked around as Max started climbing down the ladder last. She was surprised to see there were two fire engines, an ambulance and a police car all parked in a semicircle around them. There were lights flashing and people speaking on walkie-talkies.

The ambulance crew were the first to get to them. They wrapped the four kids up in big gray blankets, and helped them into the back of the ambulance. As they drove away, Ebony looked over her shoulder at the flames. They had been rescued just in time.

When they got to the hospital, they were met by Max and Hilda's parents, crying tears of relief that they had been found safe. Ebony's mom and Jay's parents were there too and couldn't thank the rescue teams enough as they bundled the Eco Rangers up in a big hug.

"They were all so brave," Dan said.

"But I think this little one was the most courageous of them all."

He pointed to Mira, who was sitting on his shoulder. Jay's mom laughed and placed the possum in the carrier she'd brought from home, while the children were taken inside the hospital.

10

Ebony and Jay gave Mira her last feed of fruit and leaf mix. *She sure is a miracle,* Ebony thought as she watched the possum race along the tree branches toward Jay. It was hard to believe it had only been two weeks since they were caught up in the wildfire. If it wasn't for Mira they might never have been found or got Hilda out safely. Though Hilda had spent a few days in hospital, they were very happy to get the call that she was doing much better now and was well enough to go home.

The possum stopped at the edge of the

tree branch in her enclosure and leaned over, grasping the piece of fruit Jay held out to her. Now they would be able to try again to release her back to the bush where they'd found her. Ebony heard a beeping sound from outside her house.

"The vets are here," she said.

Mira snatched the piece of fruit from Jay's hand and leaped from her branch onto Ebony's shoulder.

"Hey, cheeky girl," Jay laughed.

The possum nibbled on the piece of fruit, held between her two paws. Ebony patted her on the head.

"Come on, it's time to take you to your bush home," she said.

Mira scampered down into Ebony's pocket and the three of them made their way to the front where the vets were waiting. Ebony was surprised to see it wasn't just the vets standing at Jay's front door. Hilda and Max were also there.

"These two turned up at the wildlife hospital and asked us to thank you for rescuing them, Eco Rangers," Doctor Bat said.

"So, we thought we'd do better and bring them to you so they could thank you in person," Doctor Tan added, winking.

Max came over and gave Jay a high five, and Hilda raced over and hugged Ebony tightly.

"Thank you both for rescuing me from the fire," she gushed. "And thank-you to Mira, too!"

"Mira truly saved us all," Ebony said.

She held Mira out and the ringtail leaped across to Hilda's shoulder. She shrieked excitedly.

"She's clever and cuddly," Jay grinned.

"Let's release cute little Mira," Doctor Bat said kindly. "Are you ready?"

"Sort of," Ebony admitted.

"Do you need a bit of extra help?" Max

asked quietly.

"Of course, it would be special for you to be there too, since she helped rescue you," Doctor Bat said. "If that's okay with the Eco Rangers?"

"Of course! We can always use extra helpers," Jay said.

The vet van pulled up at the bush campgrounds and they all got out. Doctor Bat, Doctor Tan, Hilda, and Max followed the Eco Rangers to the spot where they'd first found Mira. Ebony took off her hairband, still wound around the log, even though it was a bit singed from the fire. Jay opened the carrier. Ebony lifted Mira out gently, and Max and Hilda gave her one last pat, saying goodbye to their little hero.

"It's time for you to go home," Jay said. "But we'll check on you every day. And I know you'll be missing that yummy fruit you like so much, so we'll make sure we bring you some."

He gave Mira a scratch on the head. Ebony placed her gently down on the ground. Mira looked at the Eco Rangers then at the large tree nearby. The base was still a bit black, but the branches and leaves had already grown back. Ebony hoped Mira remembered it was her home.

"Go on!" Jay said.

Mira stared up at them with wide brown eyes, then she looked to the tree again. She sniffed the air and then scampered toward it. She looked at the Eco Rangers one more time then leaped onto the trunk, gripping onto it with her claws. She climbed up, reaching the first branch, then crawled across it.

Ebony and Jay turned and made their way back to the vet van with Max and Hilda trailing behind.

"Great work, Eco Rangers!" the vets said together.

Ebony turned back one last time to see Mira's small face peering out through the leaves. She wiggled her nose like she was saying goodbye. Ebony nudged Jay. He looked up at the tree, smiled and waved at Mira who then disappeared behind the leaves.

"She's back where she belongs now," Ebony said with a note of sadness.

Jay nodded. "I'm going to miss her, too."

"I have a feeling it's not going to be the last of our wildlife adventures though," Ebony said.

"Eco Rangers to the rescue!" Jay said, and they bumped fists.

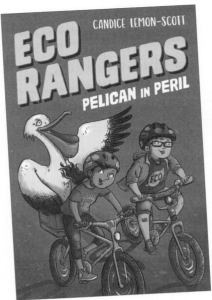

FOLLOW THE ADVENTURES OF THE ECO RANGERS AS THEY MEET OTHER CUTE ANIMALS!

OUT NOW!

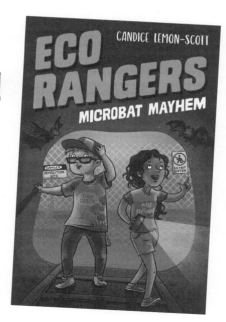

BE AN ECO RANGER!

Jay and I love caring about the natural world and wildlife animals. Here are **10 tips** to show you what it takes to become an Eco Ranger.

1. Care about nature and wildlife. Go on nature walks and spot as many animals as you can, but leave them to be undisturbed in their habitat.

2. Be curious about what's going on in the environment. Discover, explore, and read about the natural world.

3. Alert an adult or your nearest wildlife hospital if you find a sick or injured animal. Don't touch it or rescue it yourself.

4. Help with conservation work like tree-planting and litter clean-up days. It's a great way to meet other budding Eco Rangers and make new friends.

5. Make a difference by recycling everything and using less plastic. Start by picking an exciting canvas bag for your shopping!

6. Enjoy being in nature, whether it be the beach, forest or backyard. Plan exciting outdoor activities with your family and friends.

7. Respect the environment by always tidying after yourself. Never leave any litter behind and encourage people to be eco-friendly.

8. Love nature. Ask your parents if you could grow your own fruit and vegetables in your backyard or garden. It's fun and you will get to eat them, too!

9. Look after our world and write a nature diary to remember all these beautiful moments you spend in nature.

10. Spread the word about looking after nature and wildlife animals by sharing these Eco Rangers' tips with your friends!

ABOUT THE AUTHOR

Candice Lemon-Scott loves wildlife and animals and has always been surrounded by a range of pets throughout her life, including dogs, cats, rabbits, fish, birds (including a duck), and various lizards. She was first moved to write this series after helping with a couple of koala rescues from her own backyard. She continues to be inspired by her own children, Krystalin and Aliena, who love and care for nature and wildlife.

A trained wildlife carer, Candice enjoys writing about the adventures of the young Eco Rangers, Ebony and Jay. Her quirky style, fast-paced narratives, and originality appeal to young readers in particular.

Following several years working in the media, Candice now writes for children. This is her second book series.